FRIENDS WITH BENEFITS:

A Spicy Four Short Story Adventure

Ruan Willow

Dedication

This book is dedicated to lovers who play in and out of the bedroom, those who never stop playing, and those who desire to please their partners and get off on getting their partner off, plus celebrate who they truly are because that's how it should be. Openness in sexuality should be celebrated and is a blessing. Try new stuff! Fulfill your fantasies!

Mutual pleasure is mutual bliss.

This book is erotic romance, please read and enjoy it knowing this is the genre it is in.

Marinate in your sexuality daily.

Wife's First Threesome and his too: An All Virgin FMM Story

Aaron's Angel, and Mike's baby girl.

Part 1

"You seriously asked Aaron if he'd fuck us?" My heart is pounding a million times a second as my eyes widen. My stomach falls into a mash of butterflies and nausea.

"Yeah. I mean. Why not? You want it. I want it. He flirted with you in the grocery store." He laughs. "A no-brainer, baby."

I drop the package of cheese on the counter. I want this but, honestly, I'm terrified. I might vomit. "Oh my, fuck me. You mean this is really going to happen?" I chastise myself. Breathe Amanda, breathe.

I gasp as Mike grabs my butt and then whirls me around to face him. My hands land on his thick shoulders. His eyes show he's very aroused, which ticks my desire for this higher.

He pushes me against the counter. The round drawer knob hits me right between my upper ass cheeks like a butt plug, but too high. I'm pinned immobile by his hard cock pressed to my belly. My breath hitches as my clit twitches.

"Yes. So, we were sitting by the bonfire last night and everyone left, so it was just him and me, so I asked him." He grins at me before he lands a peck on my lips. "Aren't I a good husband who cares about fulfilling your biggest sexual fantasies?" His grin shows he's gloating, but he's not wrong.

"Oh, fuck. Fuck. Fuck. Fuck." My hands start to shake, and my clit sends another electric jolt through my vagina. "Oh, fuck." Can I do this for real? Fantasy is one thing, but two dicks in reality is another thing altogether.

He smiles. Presses his lips to my neck, causing me to quiver. He sucks my skin into his mouth, takes little nibbles of me that feel like they may leave a mark.

I push him away and look into his smoky grey eyes. "Has he ever cheated before? Does she know what he's doing? Do they have an open marriage? Would she swing too?" My brain swirled with even more questions, but I tried to quell the crazy in my brain.

He chuckles. "Slow down, babe. No. He said he's never done this before. But he also said Melissa hasn't fucked him in over a year, so I'm guessing swinging with us would be a no."

"No way. A year? How could she not fuck him? He's hot as fuck!" My pussy juices slither out my lips as I shift my legs back and forth. I'm reminded again of how lucky I am to have a man like Mike.

"See, I'm an enlightened man because that comment doesn't bother me in the least. I want you satisfied sexually, I just want to be a part of it too," he says with a chuckle as he presses his puckered lips to mine.

It's like he had read my mind.

"You are amazing, no doubt. I'm lucky you aren't a jealous man. But guess I'd also do a female/female/male with you and love it, so we are on the same page."

He grins. "Next on the bucket list." He ticks his finger in the air.

My nipples harden at the thought. "I'm in." I giggle. "Oh, my gosh. We're going to do this?"

"We are going to do this. We will need rules, though. Only my cock goes up your ass." Mike raises his left eyebrow, and his eyes turn stern.

"Okay, that's fine. I'm sure he won't care. He probably just wants to get fucked, not caring about the hole."

"No doubt." He shudders. "Please don't ever do that to me. A year. Fuck. I'm sorry. I think our marriage would be over."

I snort. "Fuck no. I want to fuck, you know that. I agree. I think people who aren't fucking and are in a relationship should just end it. It's not a real relationship. Or go to therapy. It's sad."

He grabs both my hips hard. "Speaking of...my cock wants to invade your pussy."

"Wait, when are we doing this threesome?" I ask as he's already stripping my shirt off over my head.

He undoes my bra. His mouth goes right to consuming my right nipple, his favorite one, even though my left is a touch bigger. I smirk as he sucks my nipple hard to the back of his throat. I moan, arching my back against the counter, barely clearing the cupboards when I lean. His free hand is grabbing at my other breast. He slowly lets my nipple pop out of his mouth while seductively holding my gaze. It's slippery with his saliva under the bright kitchen lights.

"I'm gonna spank you and fuck you right here at this kitchen counter," he murmurs. "Mmmm. Bend you over right." He growls and it explodes my passion.

Thoughts of him attacking me to paddle me and fuck me sends jolts through my clit. Dang, she's a hyper bitch today! My breathing increases as he sucks my other nipple. With no sign of intent, he spins me around and pushes my chest onto the counter. He pulls my pants down to bare my ass in a quick movement.

I gasp loudly. His aggressive mode is in full display, and the fast exposure of my ass sets my pussy drooling. I brace myself against the counter, expecting an ass slap.

His phone buzzes on the counter next to my face as his first spanking slap lands on my right butt cheek. He spanks my left ass cheek, then both. After my flinch, I read the text.

"Stop, it's him," My ass cheeks sting already. "Melissa is leaving with the kids, so he wants to do it in like fifteen minutes."

He laughs evilly before taking another slap of my ass. He snatches the phone from me.

"You naughty bastard, you had to get that last spank in, didn't you?" I snicker as I straighten up.

"Yes, baby. It gives me a giant packed hard-on, plus I love the slap sound, love your ass jiggles, love how it makes your pussy wet." He leers at me with pursed lips that slip into a grin. "What's not to love?"

I try to stifle my grin, but I fail. "Oh, stop. I know all the reasons. But if he's coming in fifteen, I need to shower. I haven't showered yet today, and I don't want to be stinky for my first threesome." I glance down at my bare tits and excitement grows in me as I realize I'm going to get to show Aaron my bare tits.

He looks at me with a confused look. "Exactly why have we waited this long to do a threesome?" He shakes his head. "Fuck. I have no clue."

"I think you thought I wouldn't, and I thought you wouldn't. So ... it just never happened." I pull up my pants and grab my bra.

"Sounds like we need to talk more because ... yeah ... this really has me hot, thinking about you as pounded-out sandwich meat between Aaron and me."

"You going to let him fuck your ass?" I giggle and start to run because I know he will spank me for that comment.

He starts after me and I run away, squealing. I make it up the stairs, zipping up faster than him because, luckily for me, he'd grabbed a can of soda.

"Your ass is mine later for that comment, baby girl." His voice is full of absolution.

I have no doubts of him making good on that threat.

I zoom into the bathroom and slam the door shut. I lock it. My heart pounds heavily and I inhale deeply to try to calm down. I turn on the water to get it hot. I bet he'd let Aaron suck his cock, though, especially if he were drunk. I bet he would. I bite my lip, hoping someday I can see that.

I get a text from Mike: Extra spanking for that comment, little miss. I'll get you, my little one.

I chuckle and look at my already red ass in the mirror.

I text back: Leave me alone. I'm showering. And it's already red.

I get another text, only this time it's from Aaron. Oh, fuck! I gasp.

Aaron: Loved flirting with you in the grocery store the other day. I'm going to come and pleasure you. I can't wait. I talked with Mike btw.

Damn, is he sweet or what? I smile at my phone. He's so sexy. I can't wait for him to suck and fuck me. I'll give him a blow job. Poor dude probably hasn't had one in over a year either, if no sex for that long. I think I'd cry my eyes out if I wasn't eaten out for over a year. What a weird bitch that Melissa. I'd fuck him every damn day. She's stupid nuts.

I stick my hand in the water and it's warm, so I step into the shower stall. The hint of bleach hits my nostrils. It's a welcome smell as I draw more of it into my lungs. The water streams down my body, the heat adding to the burn emanating from the reddened skin of my ass.

"Whew!" I'm definitely not going to be able to sit after this if they spank me more. I grin. Fuck. That's kinda hot. Spanked by two men. The stuff of my secret fantasies. Well, not so secret, since I told Mike recently.

I scrub my skin with the lavender soap and take in a deep breath. The aroma calms my muscles. I lather up my hair with clove mint shampoo, the suds slipping down my naked body in sheaths of white frothy foam. The conditioner comes out in my palm and it's white and thick. It basically looks like a wad of cum. I snicker as I splat it into my hair and work it into the strands. I rinse and lather up my anus and my pussy again so I'm deliciously lavender-scented for our threesome. I'm so excited I could pop!

I dry off as I notice I've gotten another text from Mike: I suggest you keep the hot water off your ass so it can cool down before I tan it a brighter shade of red.

I stick out my tongue and take a picture. I send it to him with a laughing emoji and the word 'Brat.'

I dry off with the thick towel as I watch the three dots dance across my phone. I chuckle before saying, "I love pissing you off, so you go ballistic on my ass. Fuck, I love to tease you."

He texts me back: Sure. Go ahead. Laugh now, you won't be when you are across my knee suffering the slaps I deliver, little girl.

I bite my lower lip as my lips spread into a smile. I text back: I'd like to see you make me.

It's not a lie.

He texts back immediately: Oh, you know I can. You've been my little girl long enough to know the punishments I can deliver. And I always catch you. Keep dreaming.

I nod at my phone. "Don't I know it." I shudder as I stare, remembering how he went all savage beast on me the first time we had sex and pelted my ass like a wild man while playing with my pussy. It had made me so wet, I was so utterly shocked that it turned me on. "Who knew daddy issues would lead to that shit?" The memory sends a big shudder through me and arouses me further.

I take a picture of my reddened butt and send it to both men with a shocked emoji face. Whoever said hints ruined sex? Certainly not me!

I open my drawer and take out my spanky butt balm. "Thank you for this, Trish," I mutter to myself as I inhale the delicious scent of the lotion. My butt calls for coconut oil, beeswax, timber, and orange essential oils. Mmmm. It soothes my irritated skin so much. "I need a bit of soothing going into this feisty tryst." I scoop out a generous dollop and smear it across my butt cheeks. I cringe slightly from my own touch. It makes my ass shine like the sun.

He texts me an emoji of a raised hand.

I finish drying off and open the door slowly in case he's there, hand raised, ready to pummel my ass. I walk along, tiptoeing to the closet as my breath comes in rapid gasps and I peer around. I'm safe. I rummage in my drawer for something sexy. Do I dress in clothes or lingerie? Never thought I'd be facing this kind of dilemma and I love it.

I tap my temple. Hmmm. Not sure what I will pick. It would be fun to get undressed by them, but it would also be titillating to just shock Aaron with something sexy and see-through right off the bat. Or I could put some sexy lingerie on under my clothes and get a bit of the best of both worlds.

I shake my fists as another text buzz comes in on my phone. "He won't quit!"

I drop my towel and dash over to the phone naked.

Aaron has texted: Wow. I've never done that before. May I spank you too?

I squeeze both my lips together in a bite. Oh, dear fuck. Love the ask! But I'm in big trouble. Two men want to spank me? I'm certainly entering a devastation zone soon. They will demolish me physically, sexually, and mentally, and I can't wait to revel in the exhaustion. It will be so luscious!

I text back: You'll have to catch me first!

The thought of two men dashing after me with passion, lust, and aggression gets my blood seething hot! "Fuck me! This is going to just slay me." I clap my hands and squeal.

"I hear you, little girl," he yells up from the main floor. "Very excited, are we?"

"Fuck yes I am," I holler down. I dance, shifting my hips back and forth. "Threesome party. Threesome party. Threesome party," I sing as I shake my booty.

"Put on something delicious for us," he commands from below.

"I will," I say. Okay. That helps. I'll put on my black laced-up thong bodice and put my black dress over the top. The bodice of the bodysuit has snaps to open it at the bottom for easy access to my holes.

I'm jittery I'm so excited. "Fuck!" I mutter.

I spray on some perfume and slather some foundation across my face. Powder up the freckles on my cheeks and forehead, and smear some glittery eye shadow across my eyelids. I apply red lipstick and head downstairs, feeling like a goddess of sex.

He whistles as I walk into the room. "Damn. You look hot as fuck. You are giving me a raging boner with that, babe. Good call on the lipstick. I want that smeared on my cock. You'd better go get it and bring it down here. I'm guessing Aaron is in deep need of getting some head, and with a smear of lipstick, too. If you are willing, that is."

"Oh, I already planned on giving his cock some mouth hugs." I bite my lower lip, then stick out my tongue, biting it as I pause my stride across the living room.

"I owe you something." He reaches for my ass and I shake my finger.

"My ass needs a momentary break, lover." I raise an eyebrow as he pouts with his lower lip out, then crosses his arms across his chest.

He grunts, rolls his eyes, then sighs. "Oh, I suppose I can wait."

I hustle up the stairs to retrieve the lipstick. As I turn to leave the room, I get a fun idea. I grab our box of sex toys, because who knows what Aaron might like to try. He may have never even tried some of these toys if Melissa is such a giant vanilla prude. We need to sex him up right.

I carry the box down the stairs and meet Mike's chuckling face.

"Ambitious, aren't you? A threesome *and* sex toys?" he asks in a voice full of doubt.

"Well, I was just thinking that maybe Aaron hasn't tried some of these and might like the chance, since his wife is a celibate vanilla ice queen who doesn't share her fun cherries or her pussy cat."

He cracks up. "Wow. You do hate her. You aren't generous at all."

"Oh, I can't even imagine how sad his sex life is. Well, lack of sex life, I guess makes more sense." I shake my head. "Have sex with your partner now because, from what my pastor used to say, we don't want sex when we're dead, so fuck now."

He laughs. "Your pastor used to say that? Laugh my ass off. I want to go to his church."

"Well, no, not exactly. I added the last part." I give him a giant smirk with my tongue sticking out.

"You saucy kitten, you. I love you." His eyes twinkle with joy and lust. He snorts. "And if that's true, I don't ever want to die."

I wrinkle my nose, which makes my eyes scrunch closed a bit. "I know. I have naughty brain syndrome."

"And you keep delightfully surprising me. You are like a deep well of never-ending fun, sexy gifts." He licks his upper lip in a slow swipe.

"You have no idea." I whistle. "I'm just getting started." Oh, I'm savoring this. Entering a new era of deeper sharing has brought the yummy kinkiness to the surface in our marriage. My eyes twinkle with excitement for our future.

"Hmmm. Well, I do hope you keep sharing, because I love experimenting with you." He strokes his significant crotch lump. "He'll be here soon. Wanna suck me before he comes?"

"No. I need to get all set up." I run my hands over all the toys.

"Tally for another spank." He shakes his head and swats the air with his hand.

I giggle. "Oh, shut up."

"Another." He licks his finger and makes an imaginary dash in the air. "You sure don't want to sit down later today, do you?"

My clit tingles into a lurch and a wave of excitement follows. I wiggle my butt at him and stick it out. "Have at it, clucker fucker."

"Oh, nice one." He pauses his walk across the living room. "Hell yeah, I'm a chick fucker. Indeed, that I am. But I know Aaron is, too. No sausage parties for us." He smirks at me as there is a knock at the door.

My clit zings with a jolt and my nipples harden as I turn and see Aaron smiling through the long glass window beside the door. I smirk because his boner is already pushing out his pants. Mmm. Fuck, this is going to be a hot rendezvous. "Nothing better than a boner delivery," I say in a singsong voice.

Mike turns to give me an amused look while pointing at his own swollen meat. "Who needs delivery?"

My pussy drools and my mouth drops open. This is a dream come true for me. This will be perfectly naughty, evil sexy yummy exhilarating, and scary as fuck… the words jumble about in my head like pebbles in a jar. And a very memorable encounter.

Mike opens the door and Aaron enters. They shake hands.

"Hey, Aaron. My man. Come in," Mike says.

"Thanks," Aaron says with the biggest grin on his face.

"We appreciate your interest." Mike closes the door behind him.

"I appreciate you guys asking me. I'm beyond thrilled. I have to be very careful about this, though." He looks behind him out the window, moving his head all about. "I'm already wondering if a neighbor saw me come in here."

"Gotcha covered. You are helping me move a dresser right now. Maybe even tell Melissa that, so it's not an awkward secret. And I'll need help again in the future too, if you are interested." He chuckles and slaps his hand on Aaron's shoulder. "I have lots of furniture to move around the house. Plus, I need help holding some boards on my deck." He chuckles. "I see you being very useful to me in the future."

"Oh, I'm interested alright. And Perfect." Aaron nods to me. "Hi, Amanda. How are you?"

"Hi, Aaron. I'm really good. Thanks for coming. You're making a sexual fantasy come true for me, for us."

"Oh, don't I know it. This is one of my fantasies, too. I figure Melissa will never do it, so I do it with you two now or die without ever having done it, and that sucks. I won't hurt her. I'm not leaving her. At this point, anyway." Aaron tilts his head with an eye flick. "Can't say I'll stay a celibate married man forever, though. Maybe when kids get older, I'll go find myself a nice wife who will fuck me every day." His expression goes from wistful to a deep shade of bliss.

"Yes. You totally need that. It's a need. Not a want." I smile at him.

"You've got that right." Aaron's eyes pierce me with want and I shiver like nails bouncing on the tile floor.

Both of their eyes are on me, direct and fierce like they want to hump the shit out of me, thoughts of which send shudders of excitement through me. I bite my lip. "How about we start with a day drink?" My skin tingles all over and butterflies jackknife in my gut.

"I could use one to loosen up. It was tense while I was waiting for her and the kids to leave. I'm a bit wound up." Aaron looks lost as he rakes his hands through his dark hair.

"Done. Beer? Whiskey? Scotch? Wine?" I take a step towards the kitchen.

"Oh, I'd love a beer," Aaron says.

"Mike?" I ask.

Mike nods and says, "Yeah, I'll take a beer too. Thank you, babe, my wonderful beautiful lover."

"Welcome." I tap my heels across the floor, making sure my hip sway happens. With sugary words like that, he's likely fixing to ask for something big. But, regardless, I love to hear it.

My hands shake as I pull two beers out of the fridge. Geez, I need a glass of wine too to smooth myself out. I pull out my open bottle of Sauvignon Blanc from last night, which has about one glass left. "Perfect," I mutter as the bottle empties right at the rim of the wine glass.

I stick a can of beer under each armpit and pick up my wine glass with my right hand, cradling the bulb of the glass in my palm, the stem between my middle and forefinger. Feeling like made in the sixties porn, I carry the drinks, teetering on a spill, to the men like a good housewife. I smile away the cringe when I see their faces.

Aaron's eyes soften as I carefully walk in my heels across the carpet towards them. He stands up and takes the cans of beer from my armpits, his fingers brushing the sides of my breasts as he does. The effect is sensual and desire flares in me. Damn, I want this man.

He keeps constant eye contact with me as he says, "Thank you so much, Amanda. You're a lifesaver." His eyes show his appreciation is genuine.

"You're welcome, Aaron." I resist winking at him because that's just too cheesy.

Mike pats the couch between him and Aaron, and I take a seat. Aaron hands Mike the can of beer across me.

My heart is beating like a train speeding down a hill, my blood surging around my body so fast, my clit is literally throbbing. This is uncharted waters, but it's been a fantasy for so long that I can't quell my excitement enough to have a poker face. I squeeze my thighs together to squish my clit and sigh.

"Mmm. Yummy sigh, Amanda," Aaron says with clear enjoyment.

"She does the thigh squeeze all the time. One of the things I love about her. She's basically a nympho." Mike's grin is lusty.

Aaron looks at me with alarm on his face.

I almost spit out my mouthful of wine but manage to get it down my throat in time before that happened. "Oh, he's not wrong."

"My wife would be pissed at me if I ever said that, but then again, I wouldn't ever say it because she's not even remotely a nympho." He releases a curt laugh before he takes a sip of his beer. Then another. And another. "Whew. That tastes really good. Day drinking at my house is a big no-no, too."

"Damn. She has a lot of rules. Does she let you have any fun at all?" I give him sad puppy dog eyes. I'd go ballistic with those kind of extensive restrictions from a partner. Thankfully, Mike is nothing like that. Perhaps I'd have left him by now, though, if he had been. I know my worth.

"Every once in a while she does, but not often. I jerk off every day in the shower, though. I did it twice already today so I can actually last." He snorts. "If I didn't, I haven't had sex in so long I think I'd cum in like thirty seconds of entering you."

"A two-shower day. Did that raise an alarm with her?" I rub his thigh. I shudder inside, thinking of living life with such a hypervigilant critical spouse. I glance at Mike again with appreciation in my eyes.

He gives me a look of wonder, but then just rubs my knee with a grin.

"No, because I worked out."

"And hey. It'd be okay if you did come that fast. I wouldn't blame you. Who could ever blame you? I just feel bad you don't get pussy at all. She at least sucks your cock from time to time?"

He shakes his head, bites his lip. "Nope. Haven't had that in probably ten years."

"Fuck no!" Mike says aghast.

"Unfortunately ... I'm serious." He shakes his head as his eyes fill with humility. "Nada."

"Alright, that's it. It's happening now. I'm giving you a blowjob." I take a giant gulp of my wine and hand my wine glass to Mike. He places it on the TV tray next to the couch with a proud expression.

"You game?" I ask Aaron, standing in front of him.

"Yes, but I'm going to tap you on the head when I need you to stop. This might make me explode a bit quickly and I don't want that to happen." He sounds too apologetic for something he hasn't even done.

"Me neither. But this is just about having fun together. So, no pressure or worries for what happens. K?" I lean over and smooth both my palms up his thighs. "Just let me know and I'll come right off you really quick." I rise to a stand again and push the bodice of my dress and the bodysuit off my breasts to expose them for him. "I adore giving head topless," I confess. Maybe he'll play with them while I suck him, and even if he doesn't, I'll get his eyes roaming them, which is a giant turn-on. This is the first time I've given a blow job to a man other than Mike since we started our relationship and it's so exciting, I might burst. My large breasts bounce as I move into position.

His eyes go big and round, his mouth spreads into the biggest grin. "Whew! Wow. Nice. Very nice. Just. Beautiful." He licks his lips and raises his left eyebrow. "Unbelievable nipples." He glances at Mike and smirks as he returns the look.

I love the collaboration in their gaze and thoughts of Mike watching me give him head rage my lust even more. My breath hitches as thoughts of unveiling his cock flood my brain.

"Thank you." My heart pounds as my nipples harden. "I'm actually really excited to blow you since you haven't had it in so long."

I kneel between his parted legs and he blows out a giant sigh when I haven't even touched him yet. Ah, poor man!

I reach for his zipper with a gleam in my eyes and unzip his pants. He leans his head back against the couch after taking another swig of the beer. "A beer and a blowjob. Now I think I'm in heaven."

"Nope. Not possible. Amanda's pastor said we don't want sex when we're in heaven." Mike guffaws, still savoring that joke.

I giggle.

"Well, this is heaven on Earth then." Aaron touches my cheek so gently, I almost cry. "Because you *are* an angel."

I cover his hand with mine and stroke it. I lean down towards his cock, the head of which is peeking out the waistband of his underwear, and a bulb of precum has birthed itself on top, just like a baby cherry.

I lick it off and he gasps. "Oh, fuck," he says. His chest curves in a recoil into the back of the couch as I lick his cock head again. "Fuck. Even that feels amazing." He touches my hair and gently strokes my scalp.

I smile up at him, making full eye contact, and push the waistband of his underwear down to expose his full swollen cockhead and shaft. I take him into my mouth, fully surrounding the very blood-packed head of his penis with the complete seal of my mouth. I push down his underwear to expose the rest of his veiny hard shaft. I glance over at Mike with Aaron's cock stuffed in my mouth and the grin on his face shows me he is enjoying watching me giving Aaron this sexual gift. It makes me feel good and so free to do a good job and enjoy myself at the same time. I soften my face and try to smile with dick in my mouth, not an easy thing to do, and then return my gaze back to Aaron's eyes.

Aaron holds my sheath of long blond curls back behind my head in a ponytail hold as I slide my mouth up and down the fat swollen head of his cock. I run my hand up and down his shaft as I suck him. My nipples harden further as they rub against the couch. The skin of his cock is firm and taut against my tongue as I slip my mouth over him. His thighs squeeze my shoulders as I work on his boner.

He's moaning so much it's making my pussy drip down my thighs. He taps my head after about a minute. I let his cock slip out and smile up at him.

"Whoa," he says. "I'm about to lose it and our fun will be over, so we'd better move on. Fuck. That was so hot, though. Oh, my fucking God." He shakes his head. "Damn. That was ... amazing." His chest is heaving which sends thrills through my body.

"Oh, yeah. She's really good at giving head. She can make me cum really fast too."

"Yeah, plus I haven't had it in forever. Fuck. Thank you. Damn. Not going to forget that any time soon." His breathing is still rapid as he cups my chin and looks me in the eyes. "You really are a damn angel, you know that, Amanda?"

"Aww. You are really the sweetest, Aaron. That was nothing, but I'm sure happy I was able to give you some pleasure orally. Geez. Ten years. That's just wrong."

"Can I ... can I ask for something? I mean, we need to talk about rules, but I love eating pussy and my wife hates the feeling of it. Could I ... could I eat you out before we move on?"

I gasp and my hand goes to my chest as confusion spreads across my face. "She *hates* it? What the absolute fuck is that about? Being eaten out makes me come. What the hell, hello, has your wife ever cum before?"

"Honestly, Amanda, I had thought so, but thinking back, I'm not sure she ever has." He shakes his head, making his dark curls wiggle a little bit, and I have the urge to run my fingers through them. "I try, but, she's just so, I don't know. Frigid, I guess is the word."

"Wow. She needs to come to see what she's missing, if that's the case. Buy her a sex toy." I point to our sex toy box. "I have recommendations."

"Oh. She'd never use it. Guarantee it. She just says she has no interest in sex." He peers over at the box with interest in his eyes.

"How about an illness? She should go to the doctor. There are illnesses that kill libido." I widen my eyes at him and nod.

"Oh, I've tried that approach. She refuses to go." He sucks his lower lip into his mouth. "So, could I? And ... I mean ... I'd love to sixty-nine too, but my hard-on won't last if we do that, and I've cum twice already today, so this will be over if I were to go again."

"I'm totally fine with that. I love watching her climax and come. So, go for it. Then, when I can't stand it anymore, I'll usher us into the next phase." Mike grins at me. He looks as if he's really enjoying directing all this.

I slip the bodice of my dress and bodysuit down to my feet and step out of it. Leaving my heels on, I scramble onto the couch and spread my legs wide for Aaron, while maintaining eye contact.

"Shaved. Nice." Aaron nods. "Naked with heels. I like it." He grins.

I slick my hand down my smooth pussy mound with a naughty grin. "All yours."

He downs the rest of his beer and sets the empty can on the coffee table, letting his pants fall to the ground as he moves. He glances back at Mike and says, "Sorry for the view of my ass." He chuckles. "Hope it doesn't kill your hard-on."

Mike guffaws. "I'm fine. Seen guy-ass a million times in the locker room at the gym. It's all good. Besides, I'm going to be looking at her, so no worries."

I giggle. "Love a good man butt discussion." I wiggle to get comfy on the couch.

Mike pulls his cock out. "I guess since we are showing parts. Can't have a threesome without us seeing each other. And really, my only rule is only I fuck her up the ass. You can put toys in her ass, but I want her asshole for me only."

"Perfectly understandable. I'm pretty much more into pussy myself anyhow." He kneels and brings his mouth close to my cunt. "You are absolutely stunning, Amanda. I love your pussy so much. Love your lips. They are just gorgeous. Really, a beautiful pussy."

He's so genuine, I almost blush. "Thank you, Aaron."

He gets a very naughty grin as he closes in on my pussy. "Gawd, I've missed eating pussy. My old girlfriend before I got married would let me eat her out for as long as I wanted. I was even known to eat her out for an entire hour. I made her cum so many times. I fucking loved it."

"Um. I might be in love here," I say with a giggle.

"I think the three of us are going to be a very good match-up." Mike's voice is low and thick with lust.

Aaron's breath lands on my pussy, making me squirm. He scoops my thighs from underneath with his hands and pulls me closer to him. His face is lit up, full of deep luscious want and joy.

Seriously, he's just precious.

He opens his mouth wide and lands square on my clit, causing me to gasp, and my torso to lurch forward.

"Mmm," he murmurs as he sucks my clit out of her hood.

I gasp and tangle my hands into his lush hair, ruffling his curls as he sucks on me. He moves to take each of my labia lips in his mouth, then licks my vaginal opening like a lollipop as he moans and groans. I writhe my legs about as he sucks. His fingers dig into the skin of my thighs as he begins to tongue fuck my pussy, his nose stabbing deliciously at my clit.

I'm moaning loudly as he migrates his mouth up to suck my clit again. He shoves two fingers into my pussy as he sucks, licks, flicks. Then he full-on sucks my clit with full strong suction so vigorously I'm thrashing my legs about. He rubs his face all over my pussy, wetting himself fully with my juices as he deeply groans. I'm loving how this man really gets into eating pussy. And I'm getting close to coming already.

"Mmm. Yes," he murmurs.

Mike moves swiftly to join us and comes alongside me to kiss my mouth. It's heavily luscious to feel his familiar mouth on mine while Aaron's is on my clit. The sensation of both their mouths on me at once sets me on fire. Mike travels kisses down to my nipples as I undulate against both their sucking of me. Mike sucks my right nipple hard and nibbles it as he fondles my left. My whole body sizzles like a lit firecracker.

I'm riding up that yummy climaxing hill fast as lightning. I whimper-moan in short bursts, then let out a long groan as Aaron nibbles at my clit. It sends twitches out three times in rapid-fire. My body jerks as he uses his teeth on me. I grab at both their scalps and press my fingers in.

"Oh, fuck, yes," I whisper. Then I moan louder and say, "Yes, yes, yes, yes, oh fuck yes, oh my Gawd I'm going to come, oh, fuck, mmmmmm." My clit thickens and I enter that zone where I know I can't stop it all from happening. I round the curve. It's coming for me. And hard.

My body bursts into the start of my climax like sun flares into the day at first daylight. I attempt but fail to collect myself before letting go, and I completely lose control as I drift into that delicious automatic response of convulsions. It grips me. My body twitches multiple times, my arms bending, my chest gyrating up in jerks as my husband suckles my tit, his mouth slipping and sliding about my wet nipple as my body moves through the orgasm. My body curls as I round the full corner of the climax into the descent of the delicious high. Aaron sucks at my pussy to slurp out my cum as I grunt out.

I moan as the contractions slow into aftershocks, my body still rocking.

I relax fully, slightly in awe. I'm frozen for a minute or so, my jaw slack. Finally, I can say, "Oh ... my Gawd." I fall silent again as they continue to caress me. "That was fucking awesome amazing to have you both on me like that." My chest is out of control heaving as I try to slow my lungs down by taking deeper slow breaths. "I mean ... wow!"

"Oh, you just wait, baby girl. Just wait." Mike stands up and says, "That was just the beginning. Now it's my turn to make you come." He's got the in-charge face on and I love it. "Aaron, would you like to spank baby girl's ass too? She's been naughty and needs punishment delivered." His grin is a rival to his lust, no doubt. He's loving ushering us to this next stage, and I love him all the more for it.

Aaron's eyes light up. "Well, I haven't done much spanking of a woman, but hell yes." He chuckles. "I'm in. I could get into that." He stands up and rubs his hands together, sporting a dangerous gleam.

My heart rate ramps up as I imagine them both going hog wild on me. Wow. That naughty grin of Aaron's ... holy fuck. It sends tingles to my body from my clit twitching yet again. "You guys are making my clit twitch."

"Good. Mission accomplished." Mike pulls me up as his face turns aggressively lecherous. "Shall we chase and attack you, or just bend you over this couch to administer your required spanks? How should we team take you, baby girl?"

I raise an eyebrow at him as I full-on shift my brain to the impending role-play. "Like I have a choice?" My heart begins to pound. I don't care how, I just want them to take me and ravage me like a ragdoll until I am drained of cum.

"Oh, you always have a choice. It's what you want. I mean, what I want, what we want, but ultimately what you want prevails. As always." He gives me a single nod. I nod back, knowing that was mostly for Aaron to understand that I've fully consented to it all. "Oh. And Aaron, her safe word is crazy. If she says that, stop immediately, as she's had too much. We don't ever want her to feel traumatized or we fuck it all up."

"Right. Got it. Crazy." Aaron nods. "No crazy needed."

"Yes, no crazy please," I say. "Maybe Let Aaron pick how I get spanked, I guess. Since we're spoiling him with new experiences." Well, truth be told, this is a new experience for us all. My clit is literally throbbing, heaving, sending out pounding throbs uncontrollably, like shards of glass flung out from dropping a jar on concrete. "I can't wait until you both get your hands on me." I can't hide my excitement. I feel my heartbeat even in my lips.

Mike widens his eyes, his eyebrows lifted. "Okay, right. Aaron, we should have a quick huddle chat here anyway to mesh out what we will do to her."

Part 2

I'm giddy. The butterflies are having a major party in my gut as I watch them talk, chuckle, nod, and fully conspire in their game plan to fully devour me. I suppress the urge to jump and clap.

I'm watching them, squirming from my comfy spot on the couch, so fucking aroused, grabbing at my tits, tweaking my nipples, rolling on the cushions back and forth as they talk. I slip off my heels in preparation to run because I think Aaron will pick to chase me.

"Hurry," I screech. "My pussy is so wet; I feel sloshy." I touch it and it's so slick, it's as if I slathered it with gobs of lube.

Mike gives me a direct look. "Okay, babe. We have a plan. We're going to sit on the couch and close our eyes. You go and hide. Your choice if you want to run and we take you down like lions on a gazelle or if you lay down like a puppy on your back and spread your legs for us. Either way, all of you is ours and we are going to spank, lick, suck, and fuck the shit out of you."

I spring off the couch, jump up, and actually clap. I squeal and take off searching for a place to hide as they chuckle at me.

"Oh, my Gawd, oh my Gawd, I can't wait!" I mutter as I scramble around looking for a good place to hide. Thoughts of being sexually ravaged in the context of feeling safe with two horny men is the most seductive thing ever. I'm so ready to have my long-time fantasy realized, my elation is off the charts.

I need a hidden place where I can sit curled up and just let my pussy drool. I can't decide. Being chased down and taken to heights of passion would make me feel the most alive I've ever felt in my life, like getting to eat the feeling an orgasm gives while it's also rocking my clit and my whole body all at once, squeezing my cream out of me like pounding on a rolled tube of toothpaste with the cap off.

"I can't wait to get fucked messy!" I call out as I slip behind the laundry room door. It always sticks out a bit from the wall, so it won't be obvious I'm here. I'm realizing my voice probably just told them where I am, but then again, I want to be found.

My heart thumps so loud I'm afraid it alone will give me away to the men. I'm just shaking, shivering with electric want.

I hear footsteps. I hold my breath.

Mike says, "I can often find her by smell alone. I'm so in tune with her scent and when she's been coming like she has just now, she gives it off pretty strong."

"Wow. Fuck. That is hot as fuck. You two are so primal. I take it hide and seek is a common fuck game here?" He clears his throat. "Fucking incredible. Man. And Geez. Fuck. You guys are showing me what I've been missing." He sounds wistful and grateful at once. "And, thanks again for sharing yourselves with me. This is an experience I'll draw on for years for jerking off."

Mike scoffs. "At least once a week I hunt her down like this. She loves it. And you're welcome. Or, you know, hey, you can just join us for years, dude. So far all is going good in my book." The footfalls stop and my body quivers. "I think she's this way. I just got a whiff."

I freeze in place. Damn. He's like a legit wolf tracking my pussy. My heart is beating so hard. I want to run away, but I also want to point my ass at them and let them pound me to another massive orgasm. Or twenty. Whoever said duality isn't seductive is a fool.

"This way," Mike says with confidence.

I peek out to watch him lead Aaron towards me.

They both walk into the laundry room, but they pass me by and go all the way into the room and peek into the exercise room that is just beyond. I react without thought, tear out of the laundry room, almost tripping over a laundry basket, dumping it sideways. I take off running across the main floor. They will get me, this I know, but the chase is what's exquisite. And being caught is even better.

My thumping heart is pounding up in my face as I run and pant in a wild panic, a scrumptious blend of delight and fear.

I glance back and both men are rushing at me. I squeal and hurl myself into the living room just as Mike catches hold of my arm. He turns me and wildly spanks my ass as I scream and try to get away, Aaron gets in a few slaps too as they both tag team spank me. My clit twitches and my pussy wets further as the smacks of their hands on my flesh fill the room. I'm ready to explode as they pull me to the couch. Mike flops me belly down on his lap and lays spanks across both my ass cheeks expertly with an open palm as I holler out. Aaron's hand migrates to my pussy and fondles my juicy womanhood. Mike keeps spanking me with aggressive slaps that make me gasp, and that send jolts right straight to my clitoris. It flings me closer to an orgasm, but then he stops.

I pout for my ruined orgasm. "Hey," I whisper.

"Mmmm, fuck I needed that. You got what you had coming." He sighs. "Fuck. My cock is rock hard. Give me a little kiss, baby girl. That was so hot." He leans back against the couch cushion with a pucker of his lips and a series of twinkles in his eyes.

I nod and plant a kiss on his lips, then I shift to suckle the head of his cock as my ass cheeks burn from the slaps. My want for their cocks inside me grows as I suck, imagining, and relishing the look Aaron likely has on his face as I give Mike a blow job. My pussy flares open. My heart tangles me into burgeoning knots as I relinquish my hold over my calm and let loose. Feeling sexually free, I bob my mouth on his cock fast and hard.

He moans and his body jerks as I suck and rub his frenulum with the tip of my tongue.

Aaron grabs my arm and my husband's cock slips out of my mouth. My jaw falls open as he bends me over the couch and lays five hard slaps across my ass. Then he rides his cock along my ass crack in a quick butt job while grunting.

"Mmm. Fuck I'm hard too. Gonna fuck your pussy with that bright red ass, baby girl," Aaron says with a deep lusty voice. He lets out a low deep man growl as he rubs his cock along my crack.

Loving him getting into this fully, my insides melt to mush.

Mike joins us. Grabbing my arm, he pulls me to a standing position and deeply French kisses me as Aaron continues to jerk himself vertically between my ass cheeks. Aaron's cock is slipping and sliding all over my ass, his hands firmly holding my hips. Mike trails kisses down my neck voraciously while manhandling my boobs. I drop my head back and Aaron's hands grab at my throat and slide up my cheeks pressing my head back further until I'm arched backwards to the max. He kisses my forehead all while rubbing his cock on my buttocks.

It's all a whirl of pleasure, lush with grabs and rubs. Their manhandling of me sends me to the brink of elation.

My mind blanks to everything but the moment as Mike mingles his fingers into my pussy—first riding them on the outside, then into me in an ever-increasing pumping, before spreading all my juices towards my clit. Mike gifts me kisses down my cleavage, slipping down my belly to fully lip massage my pussy mound. His tongue snakes into the skin cleft above my clit. With one firm hand on my hip as my body jiggles from Aaron's backside rubbing, he slips his tongue along my slit to sip at my pussy lips loudly. The sucking sounds combined with the overwhelming bodily sensations are intoxicating.

I'm sinking into the plump desire of these two men like I'm merely fog, yet being molded by both their hands and bodies into my own heavenly sensual bliss. It moves into surreal as Aaron runs his hands down my sides, then rides them back up to cup my breasts, grabbing and pinching at my erect nipples.

I moan as I'm barely needing to stand on my own as both men are holding me up as they love on me. I let myself fall limp, my want rolling me about as they both maul me, consume me, maneuver my body, hold me, rub me as I fall into an unfamiliar high. It's welcomed, and beyond luscious.

Mike flips me around, so my ass is squarely in front of him.

Aaron immediately takes my face in his hands and pushes his tongue into my mouth in a deep kiss. I kiss him back, rubbing my tongue along his, hungrily sucking at his lips and tongue. He presses his hard cock to my soft gut and my hands reach up to caress his biceps, shoulders, and firm chest. I want all of him at once.

Mike is caressing me, messing with my asshole, sticking a lubed finger in and out, riding my butthole. It's his familiar move, prepping me for his engorged cock. He slathers coconut oil all over my ass cheeks and anus. Wet sounds mean also he's rubbing it on his cock.

We fall into a tiny lull in their ravaging of me ... which only means one thing.

In a blur of skin and movement, they sandwich me. Aaron slips his hands under my thighs and holds me up. I wrap my right leg around him and Mike presses me to him, so I'm snugly wedged between the two of them. The strength of both of them is hypnotic, daunting, magnificent, propelling me to promised sexual heights I've never yet enjoyed. Aaron leans back slightly so I fall forward a bit. They both line up their cocks at my holes and Mike grunts.

"Three, two, one," he utters as my heart rages, then both enter me at once. Mike presses himself into my anus and Aaron penetrates my pussy.

I yell out as I'm sliding down on both hard cocks.

Having only been DP'd by Mike and a toy in the past, my world is split in two as they both pump into me at once. I scream out and grab at Aaron's chest, my arms flailing as my nails rake at his skin. My body is going in two directions at once, but then they begin to thrust in sync. They cock maul me as my body goes increasingly limp. I freefall into the dual submission of their hungry thrusts, launching me on a ride up my orgasmic climax at a frightening speed. It's all so deliciously dizzying, like the best sensual dream I can imagine. It's like a deep massage and a hard yummy fuck all at once. I'm gasping; they are grunting. We are three in ecstasy.

"Mmmm fuck me, yes, yes, yes, yes, yes. I'm your whore," I whisper as my body is flopped about between both of them. "Mmm. Fuck. Fuck my holes." It's barely audible, but I'm sure they've heard me as they shove themselves into me, pounding me harder. The rich, repetitive sound of the skin slapping is what I imagine must be lust in heaven.

"Mmm you fucking cumslut," Mike says in a growl. "You whore. Gonna make you cum like a faucet."

The dirty talk melts me and pushes me, along with the hard slams on my clit, and I'm gone into the oblivious high of another wonderful ejaculation.

"Fuck your pussy," Aaron mutters. "Mmm. Fuck you hard, Angel."

I'm awestruck. I love his name for me, instantly savoring being his *'Angel'. 'Aaron's Angel, and Mike's baby girl,' rings in my head as they fuck me.*

I can't even speak out to tell them that I'm climaxing, but my body jerks against them, and they both grunt and groan and pump into me harder yet as I whimper out my pleasure. The familiar pressure happens near my belly button. I have no control over my body as I twitch between them, and they ride me as I dive crash into intense vaginal contractions ...four, five ... it's too hard to count. I hum and whimper almost to the rhythm of a sob. I gasp as both still fuck me, my clit too sensitive, but I'm too spent to speak it. The pleasure may have slipped me into a sex coma as I can't even form a facial expression, but inside I'm screaming.

Aaron loses it first and he spurts his seed to paint my warm insides with his hot cum. "Mmmm fuck," he grunts.

He continues to pump as he empties his cock into me. He slows down his thrusts, but Mike is still ramming himself into my ass, and Aaron's body becomes the brace for his leverage so he can keep fucking me.

I sigh as Aaron keeps me upright, thankful that he is, because I couldn't do it. I'm still pinned between them and their cradling of me skin-to-skin is very soothing. Mike grunts and squeezes my hips, his breathing rapid, ramping up to a high pumping speed as he likely nears his climax. After a few more deep grunts he comes inside my ass.

We collapse as a unit onto the couch, all of us breathing heavily. Their skin feels sweaty, damp, as does mine.

No one speaks for several minutes, like we are sharing a moment of silence in reverence for the amazing sex we just shared.

Finally, I say, "Oh my fucking Gawd, that was utterly amazing, I mean ...wow...like beyond my wildest imagination, stellar. Holy shit. You guys were savage. And I loved it."

"Wow," Aaron says. "I mean wow, agreed. What a way to break a dry spell."

Mike belly laughs. "Umm. Yeah. I want to do that again. That fucking rocked. Blew my mind to have you thrusting into her at the same time as me. Like I could feel it." He shakes his head. "Just fucking unreal."

"Mind-blowing," Aaron says in amazement.

"I'm leaking all over the damn couch," I say with a chuckle laced through my voice. "You guys definitely fucked the shit out of me. And hard." DP wasn't what I expected, but I'd do it again.

Mike pulls me into a hug. "And you had a monster orgasm, didn't you?"

I nod, releasing a big sigh. "It was huge. I mean really huge! I lost count of how many times my pussy convulsed."

"That was the most amazing feeling. I almost lost it at that point. Never felt that before."

We both look at Aaron in shock.

"What? Ah, wow," I say as I reach up and touch his cheek.

He smiles slowly, and a satisfied look settles across his face.

"I'm so thrilled you got to feel that finally then."

"Yeah, that's made me come many times with her. Feels amazing as fuck. Completely unmatched by anything. And the aftershocks rock too."

"I was so floppy I couldn't even manage to add in vaginal squeezes before I came, I was so overwhelmed. But I totally loved it." I blow out a big breath as I run my hand through my curls. "I'd do it again in a heartbeat."

Aaron flips his limp cock about. "Same. Thank you, Angel. And Mike, you have a beautiful, sensual wife. Thank you so much for sharing her with me. If we never did this again, it was enough to last a lifetime. That was incredible. Unfathomable."

"Shut up. You are coming over in three days and we are repeating this," Mike insists.

Aaron smiles. "I'd love to be invited back. It will have to be the stars aligning properly for me to get away, though."

"Then we'll wait until they do. You could always text us when it works. We are open whenever." I laugh. "Fuck, it could even be in the middle of the night for all I care."

"Really?" Aaron asks with wide eyes. "You wouldn't mind?"

"Nah, I wake her up to fuck on a regular basis. She loves it."

"You are not cut from the same female cloth as my wife." Aaron shakes his head as he laughs. "She'd be pissed at me for weeks if I woke her for sex. She'd probably slap my face."

"I like it, actually," I say. "Being woken for sex, I mean. I love the urgency, the passion, the woozy feeling going right into arousal. It drives up our lust and we fuck hard during the nighttime. Plus, being sleepy and in the dark is kinda like being drunk, so it lowers the inhibitions."

"I don't think you have any inhibitions," Aaron says in a very amused tone.

"Oh, I do, they are just getting less and less as time goes on." I rub my temples. "I really need a towel. Will you get me one, hon?" I let out a raspberry. "I think I'm going to need to scrub all your cum out of this couch today, I'm seriously dribbling like a faucet."

"That's hot," Aaron says with a grin.

"It is, isn't it?" I smirk at him. "Thank you. I know this meant a lot to you, but it did to us too. We've been wanting a threesome for a while, but haven't found anyone it would work with."

"You are welcome. I mean, I do feel guilty, but she isn't giving me anything, so, not wanting to live a celibate life, I guess that's why I'm here." He frowns. "I want to fuck her, she just doesn't want to fuck me."

"Well. I'm so sorry for that. She is really missing out, you have killer thrust moves. You murdered my pussy." I soften my eyes. "And we're just so glad you're here. We appreciate you, even if she doesn't."

Mike returns with three towels, the largest for me.

I take it and rub it along my dribbling pussy, then along my ass crack. "Thanks for the big one."

He laughs. "Literally. My pleasure to give you the big one."

"I meant towel, ya goof," I say.

"I didn't." He sits on the couch and rests his head back on the cushion. "That was fucking hot."

"Indeed." I stand. "More beer? I want something."

"If the waitress is naked, that much the better," Aaron says as he reaches for his phone. "I have just enough time for one naked beer."

"Perfect." I shrug with a smile. My whole body throbs with delicious pings from being thoroughly worked over.

I open the fridge and grab two beers, set them on the counter. I open a new bottle of wine and again tuck the beers under my armpits and carry the wine glass.

"Much easier to walk with these without heels on," I mutter.

Aaron takes the beers from my armpits again, this time making extra efforts to touch my boobs with a grin on his face. I sit between them as Aaron passes Mike a beer.

"Now you're catching on." I raise my wine glass. "Cheers to friends with benefits, threesome fucking, and fucking doing it again."

They tap their beers on my wine glass, and we all take a drink.

"Because fucking makes you thirsty," I say as I bring the wine glass to my lips.

THE END

Finger Licking Good Threesome Roommate Rendezvous Hookup

"Lick my fingers?" Jordan asked Mariana as he presented a sauce-coated finger to her plump rosy lips.

"What?" she asked, bewildered, dropping the salad tongs.

They clanged to the floor with way too much sound.

Jordan laughed. "Well, someone has to taste it. I already did and I like it. I need another opinion." He grinned at her as she chuckled. "So, lick my fingers."

She ignored the tongs on the floor and took Jordan's fingers into her mouth. She kept eye contact with him as she did, and she knew he could see the lust in her eyes because she couldn't possibly mask it. He was so fucking sexy, and if he weren't her boyfriend's roommate, and she weren't dating her boyfriend, he'd be the next on her to-do list. He had this wave to his hair that looked styled but was natural. She'd seen it dry that way at the beach last summer. He had a body to die for and an ass she'd always wanted to grab. And this sexy man was now ordering her to lick a part of his body. Her libido couldn't take much more of this before she'd tackle him to the floor just so her thighs could encase his toned torso.

"Is it good? Or should I start over?" Jordan had been dabbling in some gourmet cooking and both Mariana and her boyfriend Sam had been benefitting from his experiments.

"It tastes good, but I need another sample." She gave him flirty eyes, which she knew she wasn't supposed to, but again, her libido had a mind of its own. She succumbed to her desire and ran her gaze down his body. He had on a dry weave, tightly fit shirt and a snug pair of jeans. He was sockless, and the aroma wafting off of him was a strong spicy one that was alluring. He'd clearly taken a shower recently, and the thought of him all wet in the shower sent a swell through her clitoris.

She had told her boyfriend recently that she'd do a threesome, but he hadn't made any moves to ask a friend. Maybe she needed to suck his cock and plead. That'd surely work.

"Okay," he said cheerfully and swiped his middle finger through the sauce.

He lifted it to her lips and held eye contact with her.

She leaned towards him, almost pressing her pelvis against his, and sucked the tip of his finger. It was time to be bold. She closed her eyes as she rode her mouth down the rest of his middle finger, taking it all the way in to the back of her throat. She attempted to rein in her gag reflex, but lost and gagged.

She fell off his finger with a raucous laugh. "Oh, my Gawd," she muttered, embarrassed.

His expression was both shocked and amused, but there was also something in his eyes that told her he liked that she'd just done that.

"Yeah," she said as she raised both hands towards the ceiling. "Gag reflex is pretty strong." She laughed at herself and shook her head. "Poor Sam, right?"

He smirked. "On the contrary." Humor filled his face as he appeared to enjoy some secret thought.

"What are you imagining?" she asked quickly, as if she had to ask.

"Something that I shouldn't say out loud."

Well, that was very intriguing indeed. She most definitely needed to know more about that thought.

Sam entered the apartment, gym bag and protein drink cup in hand. He had on a workout tank top and workout shorts. His sandy blond hair was all askew, as if he'd run his hands through it with mousse. "Whew, now that was a workout and a half."

He looked delicious to Mariana, and she instantly wanted to drag him back into his bedroom and fuck his brains out. The whole finger-sucking incident with Jordan had her randy as a swollen peach at a hungry mouth.

"Hi, Sam. Can I show you to your room?" She was not going to be subtle. He liked her aggressively coming on to him anyhow, so she never held back.

"Yes, but first, you have a bit of something on your lips." He took a step towards the two and peered into the bowl Jordan was stirring. "How's that sauce taste?" he asked with a big grin.

Her face flushed and Jordan looked amused.

She took in a deep breath, then released it. "It was ... really good." She connected her gaze with Jordan's and held it as she said, "Really good."

Sam looked back and forth between the two before catching Mariana's attention.

Mariana bit her lip, then glanced down. There was a rise of a bulge in Jordan's jeans. She was no fool. Jeans tended to mask erections, so if she could tell, it meant he had a raging boner.

"Him?" Sam asked with some surprise in his voice.

She was elated. He had paid attention. She nodded with exaggeration before she said, "Yes. Absolutely."

"Meet me back in the bedroom," he instructed with a knowing eyebrow raise. "Something red."

She skedaddled out of the kitchen with a glance back at both men. Jordan looked confused, but she simply smiled at him. She swayed her hips as she walked down the hall towards Sam's bedroom.

If he was asking Jordan to join them in a threesome, she'd gladly give him anything he wanted sexually for the next month without fuss. She'd spilled her sexual bucket list to Sam under the urge of half a bottle of wine. He had happily returned the favor and shared some new fantasies he'd conjured up recently after watching porn. She had told him she'd be willing to try them each, at least once. He hadn't seemed thrilled about a MMF threesome when she'd confided her desire for one, but now it seemed her assessment was wrong.

She searched in her drawer in Sam's dresser for something red. Her drawer contained mostly lingerie, some thongs, two tank tops, a pair of black workout shorts, and PJ pants. She needed to restock it with some items, but right now, all she needed was something sexy and red. She loved fulfilling Sam's sexual requests. She enjoyed the look of satisfaction on his face when she did as he asked. She wasn't quite sure yet if she was willing to do anything for him, but her mind was set to try most things, especially if he bought into trying her sexual whims.

She slipped into a skimpy red lace bra and panties with garters and black sheer socks that almost reached her knees. Next, she adorned her black high heels, fixed her makeup, and ate a breath mint. She laid herself out on the bed seductively. Her impatience soared as she heard the shower.

What the fuck? Sam was showering rather than racing in here to fuck her silly? That was not like him.

She considered grabbing a sex toy, because he certainly wasn't attending to her heightened arousal. She certainly didn't need him. She knew how to make herself come in about a minute and a half flat with her rose clit sucker toy.

She quickly hopped off the bed and dug in the sex toy drawer in the bedside table. Her pussy felt wet and her desire was peaking. She felt desperate and rushed as she laid back down and shimmied her panties down her thighs to expose her wanton cunt. She slopped a dollop of lube on her clit and pressed the lovely orgasm-delivering toy to her swollen bean.

Her eyes fell closed as she imagined both Sam and Jordan taking her at once on the very same bed she was writhing on. She moaned and screamed, and then squelched out a loud shriek as the toy gifted her a monstrous orgasm. Her body twitched as she rode the delicious wave.

She didn't need their actual bodies; her fantasizing about it did just the trick.

She opened her eyes and turned her head to a sound.

Both Sam and Jordan were standing in the doorway of the bedroom with boners at full mast.

"Whoa!" she exclaimed. "Holy fuck! How long have you two been there?"

"See, I told you. She's the horniest woman I've ever been with. She's an amazing sex goddess." Sam's face was full of pride and lust.

She wasn't sure she could say it yet, but she was in love with Sam. She couldn't say why she hadn't said it yet. Maybe she was waiting for him to say it, but the urge to reveal her feelings for him swelled as she took in her man. He was about to deliver her fantasy, so that pushed her button down. It was official. She was going to tell him, but not during a threesome fuck.

"Wow. She's even more yummy than I expected her to be." Jordan licked his lips and the desire in his eyes lit Mariana's passion to blazing to the sky status.

"Does this mean ... ?" She couldn't finish the question because she was panting too heavily.

"Yeah, Jordan's definitely in," Sam smirked. "As if I need to say that," he said sarcastically.

"Oh, I'm more than in. I've fantasized about this, to be honest. I've listened, and jerked, to hearing you guys fuck on a regular basis." He glanced at Sam, then at Mariana. "Sorry, not sorry. It's been kickass. You two fuck like rabbits."

Mariana guffawed as she spread her legs. "Yes, we do. Now get over here and give me those gorgeous engorged cocks. I need one in my mouth and one in my pussy."

"Yes, ma'am," Sam said.

He approached the bed first and crawled up to her, his cock bobbing as he moved forward. Jordan walked over to the bed and stood by it, pressing his pelvis towards Mariana.

"I need to feel you," Jordan said as he lay on the bed.

The two men snuggled up to her, Sam against her back and Jordan against her front.

The sandwich they made pressed her C cups firmly to Jordan and her buns wrapped around Sam's cock. He began to thrust his hardon between her ass cheeks as his hands meandered along her body. Jordan's hand slicked down her side, then cupped the side of her breast before he took her face in his hand and began deeply kissing her. His tongue spurt right into her mouth, gliding along her own tongue.

She moaned out as Jordan groaned back and she writhed between the undulating press of their bodies against hers.

"Oh, fuck, I want you both. I can't believe I get you both," she said in a breathy voice before Jordan shut her up with another deep French kiss.

They both mauled her body and she felt drunk with having four hands loving up her flesh. It was overwhelming and a rush being handled by two men at once. She twerked and thrashed against them, trying to garner as much of their touches as she could.

Sam was the first to breach her closed vulva lips. He pried them open carefully and pressed two fingers to her wet lips. He dabbed his fingers all around her vaginal opening, then dipped them in. He quickly brought his fingers to their entwined mouths and pressed his wet fingers into their kiss.

This prompted their tongues to lash against his fingers as both Mariana and Jordan tasted her juices off Sam's fingers. They both licked and suckled his fingers as he rode them around on their tongues.

"You taste amazing, Mariana," Jordan said with clear, passionate enjoyment.

Sam visited her sopping pussy again and wetted all five of his fingers with her wetness. He brought his hand back to their faces and both of them devoured Mariana's sex juice off his hand.

"I need to taste you from your pussy," Jordan declared.

He slithered down the bed as Sam pressed Mariana to lie flat. Jordan dove into her cunt like he needed it to breathe and suctioned his mouth to her fleshy womanly bits. He sucked her bean as her body thrashed while Sam took turns consuming her tits.

She writhed and moaned, quickly approaching another climax. Sam kissed her and, as Jordan took her full clit in his mouth and sucked hard, she jerked from the strength of his suck.

"Oh, fuck, I'm going to come," she said in desperation.

Sam pinched and twisted her left nipple while sucking her right.

The three-point stimulation launched Mariana into the mother of all orgasms, and she screamed. Her body fell into undulations like a puppet to her pussy contractions. A full-body orgasm descended upon her as her torso curled, her head fell back, her legs bent and rose off the bed, her toes curling.

She was a floppy rag doll soaked with sex hormones as the men positioned her into doggy position. Their grunts and growls drove her wild and raged her lust for more as they prepared to spit roast her. She wanted their cocks everywhere at once, in her pussy, her ass, her mouth, coming against her flesh, spewing spunk into her mouth. She wanted them to consume her and wring her out with so many orgasms she couldn't think straight.

Jordan pressed her cheeks and she glanced up at him.

"That's right, baby, keep looking me in the eye while I fuck your hot, tight mouth." He paused, then added, "My cunt mouthed whore."

She shuddered. He clearly had heard Sam dirty talk to her and now hearing it from him raged her lust up even more.

Sam spanked her bottom with his erection before lining it up at her throbbing slit. He penetrated her pussy while Jordan pressed his cockhead into her mouth. They both began to ride her and she thought she'd collapse to the bed. Sam's grip on her hips helped her stay up.

The skin smacks as Sam pounded his dick into her filled the room, as did his grunts and Jordan's groans.

She gagged as Jordan pushed his cock to the back of her throat and his cock twitched.

"Oh, fuck," he muttered as he sent his cum down her throat.

She gagged again, gasped and sputtered before pulling herself off his cock. She moved his cum around on her tongue.

"Quick, Jordan, get her clit. She's close, I can tell," Sam directed.

Jordan reached under her body and rubbed her clit hard, making circles around it, pressing it, mashing it as Sam railed her from behind.

She was instantly gripped by another big O as they played her G spot and clitoral head at once. She twitched and yelped as she came. As she collapsed to the bed, Sam drilled her on repeat, pounding her down into the mattress.

He came with a roar, still pumping his seed into her as he drained himself into her contracting internal walls.

The three of them fell to the bed, all three panting.

"Oh, wow," Jordan said, the first to speak. "That was the best in my life."

Mariana nodded and weakly whispered, "Same." She gasped, trying to slow her breathing down. "It was the best fuck of my whole life so far." She took in a deep breath and released it. "Thank you both. Just wow." She curled towards Sam and kissed him on the lips. She held eye contact with him and mouthed, "I love you."

He grinned big and mouthed it back.

There. They'd both said it and it felt glorious to Mariana. "You are the best boyfriend on the planet."

"I think the best on the planet applies to you, my sweet babe," he said as he caressed her face.

"I believe we need to grill up those wings. We are all famished after that." Jordan rose off the bed and made his way to the door. "Thanks for having me. And if you ever invite me again, the answer will always be yes."

He left the room and closed the door behind him.

"You really are the best boyfriend in the world for giving me that."

"Well, you've agreed to try my fantasies, so I could only return the favor."

"I'm so happy seeing Jordan naked didn't turn you off." She snuggled into his warm body.

"You are sexy enough to keep that from happening, babe." He held her close and kissed the top of her head.

"I guess we have a new fuck buddy, huh? And how convenient he happens to live in the bedroom next door!" she said with excitement.

"Oh, he was so happy when I asked him. You should have seen his face."

"Confession," she said sheepishly. "I sucked Jordan's finger." She cringed, hoping he wouldn't be mad.

"I know, he told me. We are good friends, and he didn't want to ruin our friendship, so he confessed. He said it started out innocent, but then turned hot."

"Yep, that's exactly how it happened. I didn't mean to, but it was so erotic sucking that sauce off his finger, I couldn't help it."

"Hey, I want you to have as much pleasure as possible, and I know you want that for me."

"Oh, I do!" she insisted.

"Good. Then we match."

She grinned big as she pressed her forehead to his. "We do. I love you."

He smiled back. "I love you." He sighed and caressed her cheek. "Lots of new ground covered today."

She nodded. "Yep. And good ground."

"I agree. Now let's go help our new friend with benefits make our dinner."

"I'm so ready for it all."

"You realize this now means you will be in the vicinity of two very horny men most hours of each day."

She jumped as a giddy expression overcame her face. "Yes! And I'm the luckiest woman alive!"

The End

Waking to His Alarm Cock

Zane watches as Maria and Lissa sleep. Both of them came so hard that last round before bed that Zane cheered when they both conked out. He couldn't ever get enough of his girlfriend and her friend. The sex-with-benefits had started four months ago, when they were all high. They'd been drinking and smoking all night, and then a joke turned into a dare and Zane got the women to kiss. They were plastered enough to take his suggestions and encouragement, and soon they were tribbing right on the couch.

That had been the first of many threesome trysts they'd succumbed to, and now it had become a regular thing. Zane glanced at the pile of uniforms on the floor. Maria had worked three doubles in a row at the hospital. She needed this sleeping in so bad.

Lissa had been stirring a bit, but he didn't want to jostle the bed too much for fear he'd wake Maria. The cock barrage he'd given both women not more than four hours ago should have been enough to keep his dick a noodle for a long time, but there he was, sporting a morning wood, anyway. It was like any time past 4:30 am and his cock flared like a wild bleeping beacon. Quite the alarm cock to wake up a horny hot mess every morning. He grinned. He had an alarm cock, he didn't need an alarm clock. Maria never complained because he made her come every morning, too.

Lissa opened her eyes fully and waved at Zane.

He waved back. Lissa was a kindergarten teacher at their daughter's school. If anyone spilled the beans about the three of them fucking, she'd said she'd lose her job. He had zero intention of putting her at risk because he loved their threesome arrangement. The hardest part was keeping their daughter, Morgan, from catching Ms. Hathoway in mom and dad's bedroom. She was young, but that was just too unusual for her to dismiss, so they'd been careful to be sneaky.

Lissa pointed at Maria, closed her hands together, and put them under her cheek.

Zane nodded.

Lissa smiled. She stabbed her cheek with her tongue and closed her hand in a fist and pumped it in front of her face.

Zane nodded aggressively.

She carefully got off the bed and tip-toed around it.

Zane felt his cock thicken as she approached. She stripped her top off so her tits were bare and she laid upon Zane, readying herself to give him head.

She quickly took him into her mouth. Her nipples were solid peaks. As she bobbed on his swollen cockhead, her tits bounced. Her eyes went wide as she took his cock deep.

Zane loved that she liked to choke on his cock, and he really loved it that she had throatgasms. Maria never went there. The bonus of the situation was, what one woman didn't do, the other did, so Zane was always one happy man. Maria would do anal, but Lissa wouldn't. Maria was dominant to Lissa, and Lissa was submissive to both Maria and Zane, Zane being the most dominant of the three.

Zane's body curled as Maria gagged on him. He almost lost his gizz, but she popped off his dick and grinned up at him.

"Almost," he whispered.

"I know," Lissa said. On her knees, she pointed her big ass in the air and wrapped his cock up for a titty fuck. She rode him until he held her body tight and thrust his cock up into her cleavage.

They both were grunting, and the bed was jerking, but still Maria slept.

Zane had plans to talk with both women today about considering a full-time three-way relationship. The only way he figured they could make it work was if Lissa moved into their basement and 'rented' a room. This would not be tough to do, but the biggest challenge would then be to keep their daughter from catching them all sleeping in the same bed every night.

Zane clenched, trying hard not to come. He shook his head at Lissa as she raised an eyebrow with a teasing look in her eyes.

"Want your come," she insisted.

He shook his head. "No, I want to fuck you, and I may not stay hard after last night."

"Oh, I'll get you hard," Lissa said confidently. "I'm up for that challenge."

Maria finally stirred in the bed and opened her eyes. "Oh, my. This is quite the way to wake up. Do I get to play, too?"

"Fuck yes, you do, babe. Come here." Zane pulled his high school sweetheart to his body and kissed her on the forehead. "Get enough sleep? You were so worn out."

Zane's body crumpled as Lissa sucked him hard. "Damnit, fuck." He bucked Lissa off. "You are determined to make me come, aren't you?"

She nodded vehemently, her red curls bouncing and her pink-tipped tits shaking. "I'm hungry for your cum. Morning cum always tastes the best."

Zane hadn't ever heard that one before, but he was not complaining. "I'd love to see a muff dive first. How about you two make each other come, then you can have mine."

Maria squirmed and stretched. "Mmmm. I'd love an orgasm. Lissa, what do you say? Let's make each other shake."

Maria spread her legs and Lissa hovered above. The touchdown of their pussies was always something Zane loved to watch. Their reactions to warm pussy on warm pussy were always so damn delicious.

"I'll read you two a little snippet I wrote yesterday and you two act it out, okay?" He'd taken to writing some erotica and started publishing it on Medium. He'd been really enjoying it, and he knew this was going to be a fun hobby, and he'd go as far as he could with it. Writing had always been an interest to him, and doing construction during the day was about as far from erotica as he could get. This was helping him use other parts of his brain and sexuality, and the satisfaction level was becoming a dream come true.

"You need to get into 69 position for this, though," he instructed with relish. Watching them simultaneously eat each other out was even more arousing to him than them tribbing.

The women lined up mouth to pussy with lecherous, lusty looks.

"Mmmm, fuck yes," Zane said as he stroked his engorged cock. "Yes, more of that."

The women suctioned their mouths to each other's lips and began the mouth ride.

"Rub your chin across her moist petals, inhale her gush as you dive into her. Tongue molest her sensitive bits to make her twitch and scream as she gropes your hair, your head bobbing between her thighs." He paused as they made mouth smacks and yummy moans. "Consume her very essence as she comes with such ravishing that her body curls you up." He scrolled through the notes app on his phone for another one to read to them. "Nipples so pale pink, the color ripens to deeper hues — moist saliva-tipped nips — as they harden in between blankets and fingers. The calm barely hung on as their lust began to rage its fiery head like a flaring piston — it raged like fireworks in the night, screeching along like spilt cum in morning sunlight. Their sweaty bodies flopped together as they came. With dewy lips and gasping lungs, they laid satiated in the afterglow, her clit twitching with aftershocks."

Maria's body gyrated first, then within thirty seconds Lissa's hungry libido met her climax. Both women's bodies shuddered. He loved it when their orgasms overlapped.

They both moaned out and fell flaccid, with happy looks smeared across their beautiful faces.

Zane rose up and got on his knees. "My turn." Without a glance at the clock, he situated himself between Maria's thighs and penetrated her wet, lush cunt in a flash. He sank right in and both of them groaned.

He rode the love of his life hard, making sloshy smacking sounds as he fucked her while Lissa gobbled her nipples. Maria reached under Lissa and played with her clit. Zane harnessed his control and held off coming as Lissa came from Maria's clit spanks, then he banged Maria until she was near climax.

He pulled out and demanded in a stern voice, "Doggy."

Maria scrambled up and flipped over, quickly arranging herself on her hands and knees. Lissa knew what to do. She grabbed the big black vibrating dildo and aligned herself on her hands and knees next to Maria.

Lissa handed Zane the dildo and he penetrated her slit with it. He pumped the toy into her aggressively as he thrust himself into Maria. He fucked both women until Maria's body shook with another orgasm, then he pulled out and slid over to fuck Lissa.

Maria lay crumpled, face down in the bed, whimpering as he pounded his hard cock into Lissa. She exclaimed as she came, her contractions on his cock pushed him over the edge and he came explosively in her pussy. He knew she wanted a baby, and though no one had acknowledged it, they weren't using birth control. He let his cock slip out of her with a smile.

"Good job, baby," he said as he stroked her bottom.

She crashed down to the bed and cuddled into Maria's arms.

Zane snuggled up behind Lissa, spooning her before finally glancing at the clock. Morgan didn't have to be up for an hour, so it was time for a cum soaked morning nap.

Zane happily smiled as he dug his nose into Lissa's lush, sweet-smelling curls. Could he be a husband to two women? He sure thought he could. He settled in as his eyes fell closed.

Bliss. This was pure bliss.

The End

The Accidental Threesome, Roommates Who Finally Had Some Fun

"Show us your tits," Dan yelled from the living room.

Asheley froze in place, the piece of lettuce in her hands first quivering then descending to her sandwich. She'd been desiring such a request from Dan since they had met last year. Becoming roommates with him and Anders had brought her to believe they'd hook up, but after four months, still nothing. But now, there was this request.

"Yeah, look at that shirt, her tits are about to pop," Anders said with a voice brimming over with want.

Asheley frowned. Of course, they hadn't been talking to her. That was wishful thinking. They respected her too much. That was part of the problem. No one ever took a chance on her, and she just sat in her room masturbating with toys and porn when she had been living with two dicks for months.

Maybe she needed to make it known she was open for play, but she hadn't figured out how to say it without losing their high opinion of her. The three of them were buds. They ate together, worked out together, went to parties together, and watched sports together. In all that time, neither one of them had made a pass at her.

She knew she was sexy, glances from men daily told her she was desirable, but all the guys seemed to think of her as a friend. She'd gotten permanently friend-zoned in their group of friends, and it sucked ass.

The truth was, she'd be using Dan's comment to masturbate in her bedroom in a few minutes. She imagined herself standing in front of them as they said that sentence to her, and her clit lurched a twitch. She'd dance and tease them, then lift her shirt to show off her gorgeous boobs. And she had gorgeous boobs! Only no one ever saw them but her.

She continued to make her sandwich. A boring lunch to match her boring as fuck sex life.

Dan cheered from the living room. "Ah, fuck yes! I knew she'd have the best tits on the planet!"

That too was a line she craved to hear him say to her. She didn't feel guilty about wanting to objectify herself in front of them, she wanted them to desire her. No matter how scantily she clad herself around the apartment, loose tank tops showing side boob, tiny shorts, and even going pantless, nothing worked. No ass grabs, no titty claims, not even an accidental brush-up while cooking together in the kitchen.

She'd fantasized about walking around nude. What heterosexual man could resist that, right? With her luck, they'd probably hand her a towel and avert their eyes. She was the sister, the buddy, the 'just another guy'.

Only she wasn't any of those things.

Anders belted out, "Aw, yeah, fuck her good."

Porn watching with them had also become too agonizing. The last one she'd watched with them, she got so horny she fled to her room and fucked herself into twelve orgasms. It just wasn't fair. Living with two sexy men should mean some sex, not celibacy.

College dorm life last year had at least gotten her a few hookups, but this year had been dry as a Sahara on water pills, nothing juicy about it at all.

She glanced into the living room as she walked towards her bedroom, and the scene on the screen was a threesome. Of course it was a threesome. The woman was getting railed from behind and taking a mouth fuck. A spit-roast scene to aspire to because her face was plastered in bliss. She sighed as she attempted to view their crotches from behind the couch. That had been the other painful part of watching porn with them. They both always had raging erections.

"Ashe," Dan called while glancing back. "You gotta see this one. Eat your sandwich. Here, I'll rewind it for you. It's epic, especially when she gets a titty fuck and a butt job at once." He cackles. "Dudes were riding her crevices like fucking jockeys on steroids. Her body was flopping all over."

Asheley felt her arousal rage. She almost dropped her plate when Anders stood up because he had gray sweatpants on, and was sporting a precum wet spot.

"Fuck," she muttered under her breath. It didn't help that she hadn't had sex in eleven months, not since breaking up with Manny.

"I need a beer. Dan? Ashe?" He started to move and his cock wiggled.

Asheley's jaw dropped. It looked as if he had no underwear on with how easily his erection shifted beneath the fabric. Literally weak in the knees, she simply shook her head and ambled down the hall.

"Ashe, what's up? How come you don't watch porn with us anymore?" Dan called after her.

She froze in place, her heart pounding. This was her chance to say something, but she was terrified to. "Um. I don't know. Was just going to eat my sandwich."

"Eat it out here, for fuck's sake, Ashe. We haven't spent any time together in the past few days. You keep hiding out in your room."

"Yeah," Anders said as he sauntered across the room, two beers in hand. "Come watch with us. Or maybe you get too horny," Anders said with a snicker. "Makes you want to fuck." He burst into laughter. His face showed he was clearly just razzing her.

She'd often wondered if they heard the hum of toys coming from her room. I mean, how could they not? The other day she used her super loud one, hoping they'd bring it up, or tease her or something, anything to acknowledge it would have been hot as fuck. But she got nothing.

She froze in place with her mouth ajar. Her face reddened, and she couldn't stop her nerves from rattling her resolve. She knew she looked nervous, but it was too late to make her face blank.

"Wait, what?" Dan asked, sitting up straight.

Anders stood in front of the couch, about to take a drink from his beer, but remained motionless.

"Ashe?" Dan asked again, standing up. "Cause if you ever want to fuck, oh my God, I'd fuck you anytime you wanted me to."

Anders nodded dumbly. "Same. I guess I assumed you just saw us as friends, but truth be told, you drive me fucking crazy on a daily basis."

Dan guffawed. "Yeah, same. And when I hear your toys going, shit ..." He dropped off mid-sentence, but no other words were needed.

She wanted to cry and jump for joy at once. This meant they hadn't friend-zoned her, she'd friend-zoned herself. She stumbled over her words as she said, "I ... well ... but..." Then she smiled deeply as her inner sex kitten oozed herself to the forefront of her. "I actually fantasize with those toys, about you guys fucking me. It's why I can't stomach watching porn with you anymore. I want to fuck too much, and I can't tolerate sitting in the same room with you two."

"Get the fuck outta here. Are you being actually serious right now?" Dan's eyes widened and his expression was set in utter shock.

"It's true." She sashayed her hips as she walked down the hallway towards them. "I do want you guys to fuck me. I thought you thought of me as just another guy."

Dan and Anders both burst into laughter.

"You? Just another guy? Do you even realize how sexy you are? Come on, this is just ridiculous. We talk about you all the time." Dan ran a hand along his erection and shook his head. "You have no idea."

"Well, no one bothered to tell me!" she said, aghast. "I might be the one to tell, ya know." She knew she was coming off sassy, but it was too strong to quell.

"I'm game," Anders piped in quickly.

"Ashe, put your sandwich in the fridge and let's talk. Because, seriously, I'm in too, if that's what you want."

"I need to eat, so I'll eat while we chat." She grinned as she joined them in the living room, choosing a recliner across the room from them so she could see their faces while they discussed fucking. She couldn't wrap her head around that this was legit happening. She'd partied with these two all last year. They'd had a blast their freshman year, even played basketball and volleyball, and they often lifted together. How this had never come up before literally made zero sense to Ashe. She tried to process the fact that he had admitted they'd talked about her in a sexual sense, so how this was literally the first she was hearing of it? Her mind was blown, and they hadn't even fucked yet. How much of a mind explosion would it be to actually fuck them?

Her mind reeled as she took the first bite of her sandwich, realizing the sexual energy of the room had just skyrocketed, and she'd likely not make it through her sandwich before she had one, or both, of their cocks inside her somehow. The thought of which titillated her, making her pussy juice wet her nether lips. She shifted in her seat to test it and knew if she slipped her fingers inside her hot slit, they'd get slicked.

She started speaking before finishing chewing. The excitement of their impending hookup was too much to wait on. "Yes. I can't watch," she paused to finish chewing, "porn with you guys because it makes me too horny." She licked her lips and shook her head. Sometimes men seemed too dense to be created of the same stock as women. "Haven't you noticed me tear out of here every time we do? For fuck's sake. I thought it was obvious." She tried to temper her tantrum.

"No, I just thought you were done, or wanted to, I don't know, go fuck yourself or something," Dan said with bewilderment. "And so all this time ..."

"We could have been fucking," Anders finished.

She nodded as she chewed another bite. She smirked because stuffing her face in front of them was not exactly arousing. "I'll finish this later." She scurried to the kitchen and swiftly slipped it into the fridge, downing some water before returning to the living room.

Both of her roommates still held expressions of confusion and surprise. But she also saw lust in their eyes, so she gave a seductive look back to both of them as she nestled back in her chair. "We'd need ground rules."

They both sat very attentive to every word.

"Of course, we are still friends." Dan's face spread into a smile. "Is this going to really happen? Legit?"

Asheley couldn't stop her own grin as she nodded. "I've wanted this for a long time, but felt I couldn't ask. Plus, I didn't think you guys were interested in me that way."

"Shut the fuck up," Dan said jokingly. "Well, shit, ...all this wasted time."

Anders turned serious. "We're talking just fucking, right? Not like we will be boyfriends and girlfriend?"

"Precisely," Asheley said with absolution. "I don't want a boyfriend. That's not what I'm wanting to do now. I just want sex. If you guys are in."

Both of them stared at her in dead silence.

It lasted for too long and she stood up. "Never mind." She started out of the living room, and Dan stood up to stop her.

"Don't leave. This is like every guy's dream to hear from someone like you. And I'll fuck you as much, or as little as you want, and ask nothing more of you. If you want to stop, we stop. It changes nothing."

Asheley knew that was a load of crap. It would change everything. But she welcomed the change, and desired it.

"Deal," she said as she uncrossed her arms and unfurrowed her brow. "And I don't do anal, so double action will be tit sucking and eating me out, spit-roasting, sucking and hand jobs, or maybe double V, which I haven't done yet." She said it so matter-of-fact that it didn't even seem like she cared, but that wasn't true at all. She relaxed her stern face and added, "And, yes, I want to do this with you two very much."

They both approached her and her heart jumped, then began beating as if she were dashing off down the hallway. Her breath caught in her throat and she made a garbled sound that made her feel awkward as fuck.

"Can't wait to see your O face," Dan said as he touched her arm.

"If I say frog legs, stop whatever you are doing." She smirked as they laughed at her choice of safe words.

"You got it," Anders said as he caressed her other arm. "Living with you, seeing you as sexy as you are every day had been torture for us."

She was filled with pleasure at the sexy compliment. Her cheeks flushed and she scrunched her shoulders. It felt so good to hear him say this, she'd felt unsexy for months and months. "Really? I had no idea. And compliments get you everywhere."

"Everywhere but your ass," Dan corrected with a cackling heckle.

"Right," she said, pointing at his face. "Not into butt stuff."

"Well, no one's perfect," Anders said jokingly.

Their relationship was such that his comment wouldn't even come close to offending her. Plus, she was very confident in her wants and desires, so she didn't give a fuck if they didn't like it.

The porn ended on the screen, and another one began to load. Anders pushed the button to keep it going, then spun Asheley to face Dan. He pressed his generous hard-on to her buns as Dan caressed her arms.

Leaning in to give her a peck on the lips, he asked, "C?"

She nodded. "Yep, you guessed it."

"Knew it," Anders blurted.

"I knew it. Confession time. I've looked at your bras while they were drying in the bathroom."

She belly laughed. "Then you didn't really need to ask me, did you?"

He shook his head as he pressed his open mouth to hers and kissed her deeply.

"Mmm, ham and cheddar?"

She giggled with a nod before he kissed her again.

Anders slipped his sweatpants down and she felt him rubbing his erection between her ass cheeks. She was totally okay with that kind of butt stuff, as long as they stayed on the outside. Any poking in, and she'd say 'frog legs'.

As if he had read her mind, he asked, "This okay for you? You have the best bubble butt on campus, you know."

She snickered before Dan cupped her breast and kissed her neck.

"I'm good. If you don't hear me say it, you're in the clear." She paused. "And ribbit means you'd better slow the fuck down before I smack you."

"Got it," Dan said as he fondled her breasts. "I'd expect nothing less from you. And I can't wait to see your nipples."

Having both her roommates groping her and thrusting their cocks against her torso sent her into a rage of desire. She felt her crazy side rise to her surface. She knew she was going to blow their minds because all of her exes had told her she was an animal in bed. Not that she'd needed them to tell her.

"Remember her nipples at the pool party when she forgot a swimsuit?" Anders asked suggestively. "You kind of already know."

She remembered that pool party from last summer. She'd forgotten a suit and was going braless because the tank top was supportive. She'd just swam in the shorts and tank top. But she didn't recall either Dan or Anders ogling her that day, but she also remembers getting plastered. She laughed inside. Of course, she hadn't noticed. They were likely so expertly covert at ogling her that she had completely missed it altogether. So, they were even, and all damned oblivious. She hadn't picked up on their interest, and they hadn't on hers. It was an even starting ground for friends with benefits.

Dan pulled her tank top straps down and slipped the fabric off her breasts. Anders quickly came around the front just in time as her breasts popped out.

"Oiy, fuck me," Dan said. "Fucking perfect tits, Ashe. Fucking perfect."

She smiled with pleasure. She'd imagined him saying that so many times, but nothing beat actually hearing him say it to her face.

"Thank you," she said as her insides melted. Confirmation that she was sexy after all was very satisfying. She wasn't about to admit low confidence to them, though, that wasn't sexy at all.

"Hot as fuck tits, Ashe. Fucking spectacular."

She beamed a smile at him as both men grappled her breasts.

"Wow," she muttered as they both molested her tits.

Anders was the first to take a nipple in his mouth.

She moaned without thought. As she writhed between both men, giving ample attention to her breasts, she realized an interesting phenomenon. The arousing effect of having her nipples suckled and played with was rivaling the excitement she was enjoying that it was Anders and Dan who were doing it. She was used to having boyfriends do this to her, even strangers in her few spontaneous stranger hookup fucks, but it was somehow an entirely different thing to have her two best friends enjoying her boobies. And it was taboo, which made it even more delicious.

"Oh, don't stop, please," she pleaded.

This made both of them go even harder at her body. She gasped and felt weak. She'd snuck peeks at both of their erections, but to have them pressed to her now, and them thrusting them against her, was satiating all by itself, and no one had even broached her clit yet.

She sighed and allowed them to manipulate her body into undulations caused by them each sucking, pinching, twisting, and squeezing her breasts and nips. It was an all-out foreplay feast of tit play. She hadn't even come close to realizing how much they'd been enjoying looking at her tits all this time, but the way they were devouring and playing with them proved it.

As Anders went back to thrusting his cock in her ass crack, Dan was the first to slip his fingers into her waistband. He hooked his fingers under it and gently slid her workout shorts down. Anders took a step back and helped the shorts slide down her buttocks. He knelt down and delivered a small bite to her right ass cheek.

She squealed in delight.

Dan nuzzled her ear as he whispered, "Seeing you commando all the time has also driven us crazy."

She smiled, thrilled they had noticed. She had done it for herself, but she wasn't going to lie, she loved that they had observed her going frequently without panties.

"You noticed," she cooed.

"How could we not? It's sexy as fuck." Dan caressed down her tummy, then crested her bald pussy mound. "We're gonna have so much fucking fun."

She tittered a laugh in agreement. "Yes. Yes, we are." It was also gratifying to know they'd talked about her going commando. That thought ramped up her desire for them even higher.

"Morning sex or night sex?" Anders asked.

"Yes," she retorted in a sassy voice.

"You may not ever return to your own bed." Dan cupped her hips as he pressed his fingers into her flesh.

Having a bare pussy and ass in front of them felt naughty and yummy at once.

"You won't hear me complaining, as long as your mattresses don't suck." She released a long appreciative sigh as Dan parted her pussy lips to slip a finger into her hot slit.

"Only sucking there will be on us or on you. My mattress is new this year." Dan kissed her mouth as he began to finger-fuck her.

She slouched, almost crumpling from how their touch was stimulating her. Four hands and two cocks on her was much more overwhelming and brilliantly exciting than she had expected. She felt woozy as they played with her body, pushing all the buttons, even ones she hadn't been aware of before being with two horny men.

Anders kissed her shoulders and back, then licked down her spine, which caused her to squirm in astonishment. He rounded out his tongue ride by licking her buns all over. He pressed his fingers to the back end of her slit and started to press his fingers in. A double finger-fuck was filling her up quickly and sending her desire for a cock to inferno level.

She knew why they'd arranged themselves this way. Dan was a boob man, and Anders was an ass man. She'd watched so much porn with these two that she had elucidated info about their sexuality from their reactions, as likely they had of her as well.

"We're going to fuck you into so many orgasms you scream, Ashe," Dan said while maintaining eye contact with her.

"Please," she said in a meek, humble voice. It was already getting difficult to converse with how hard she was panting, and how much the ecstasy was filling up her brain.

Anders gripped her shoulders and spun her around, and his mouth was on hers so fast she had barely taken another breath. Dan kissed down her neck and mashed her fleshy butt between his large palms. Ashe had watched him palm a basketball so many times, and had yearned for his big mitts grinding on her big bottom. And now that it was happening, she loved his touch so much. She almost slithered to the floor like she was a boneless puddle of hormones. And then there was Anders, sucking on her erect nipples again and playing with her clit.

"Spit-roast?" Anders asked when he had released her tit from the tight suck.

Dan was finger-fucking her so hard she couldn't think. Each thrust into her, his thumb would smack against her swollen bean, and she'd cry out in pleasure.

Anders grabbed both tips of her tits and twisted them while chanting, "Tune in, Ashe. Tune in, Ashe. Can you hear me?"

She buckled with laughter and nodded aggressively. "Yes," she whispered.

"Good." He nodded to Dan, who pressed Ashe to a bent-over position.

This was it. She could now die happy having been taken in a spit-roast by her two friends. She was getting so aroused, she knew it wouldn't be much longer before she'd come.

Dan ran his cock along her labia lips, then penetrated her cunt slowly. She groaned, as did he, and his thrusts into her began slow, but sped up quickly.

Anders held her face with one hand, and fed his cock into her mouth with his other. He began light thrusts as her gag reflex reared its head. She'd never been spit-roasted and the dual pounding of both their hard cocks into her sent her into a flight of hormones zipping around her body the likes of which she'd never enjoyed.

She gagged, but Anders kept going.

First Dan growled, then he began to rail her relentlessly, beating her generous butt cheeks into constant gyrations. She had a pretty big butt for an athlete, or so she'd been told.

Anders grunted next and skated her higher towards a climax.

She slipped off Anders's fat dick and muttered, "Clit."

Dan immediately responded and rode her clit hard with his fingers, while still pumping himself inside her.

Her ecstatic realm swirled up from her gut and exploded across her body as she peaked in an orgasmic climax. Her body jerked. She gagged and fell off Anders's cock as her body twitched its way through the delicious and intense climax. The contractions bounced out of her female center and squeezed Dan's dick on repeat.

He shouted out as he pulled his fingers from her clit to grip her hips and rail himself into her. He came with a roaring yell.

Quivering and almost falling, Anders swiveled her body so her ass was pointing his way, and he shoved his cock up her so fast she gasped and sputtered.

With the taste of Anders's precum on her tongue, he rode her hard and fast into his own orgasm.

She knew her friends were clean, and she had birth control covered, so there was nothing but the pleasure to savor as the three of them landed on the couch. With Ashe in the middle, she placed her hands on both their thighs.

She drew in a breath and released a big sigh. "Now, that's more like it. Watching porn together now needs to be done while fucking."

Anders laughed and Dan snorted.

"Good plan," Dan said with relish.

"I'm always in."

"Do we get to use all those toys on you?" Dan asked with hope.

"Absolutely. I'd be bummed if you didn't."

"Fuck, I can't tell you how many times I've masturbated to hearing you use those things." Dan rose from the couch, his cock half-flaccid.

"Same. And Ashe, we used to talk about it. And when you'd make sound, oh fuck, I'd spurt my cum like a fountain." Anders held her chin. "I'm not kidding, babe. It's true."

"Wow, and here I thought I was just another guy to you guys."

"Not possible," Dan said as he returned with three beers and Ashe's sandwich.

"We are going to have so much fucking fun going forward, and I finally got to see your naked tits," he declared with glee.

Ashe laughed. "And I got to see your cocks. We might not get any more schoolwork done 'cause we'll be fucking."

They tipped their beers together.

"Cheers to fucking," Ashe stated.

"Cheers to all the fucking," Anders agreed.

"Cheers to tasting each other's cum." He paused. "But not yours Anders, I'll leave that to Ashe."

"I'm in!" Ashe said with exuberance.

They enjoyed each other's company and made a date for the evening to meet in Dan's bed, and Ashe was to bring every toy she owned.

The End

Ruan Willow

About the Author

Ruan Willow is an erotica author, sex blogger at https://ruanwillowauthor.com/ , sexuality and erotica fiction podcaster at the Oh F*ck Yeah with Ruan Willow Podcast, and an audiobook narrator/voiceover actor. She is also published on Medium, Frolic Me, and Literotica. She loves spending time with family and friends, interacting with fans, cooking, sharing/chatting with and educating people about sex, reading, travel, being outdoors, swimming, learning about sex, podcasting, and more sex. Did you catch all the sex? She's giggling right now thinking about you reading all about sex. She values openness and talking about the natural act of sex. And. Yup, she loves to laugh!

Thank you!

Thank you to all my family and friends who support me. I wouldn't be where I am without you. You are all the magic and the light in my life, the love that grows in my love. I am honestly thrilled and humbled by the supportive people in my life. Love you!

To Fans:

Thank you for purchasing and/or reviewing this book!

I peddle fantasies for the purposes of your enjoyment, entertainment, and expanding your sexuality and openness. Always remember that no fantasies are bad. You should enjoy your sexuality and your fantasy life as much and as often as you can.

Thank you for reading my book! I write for myself and for my fans. My fans are my main focus though, but of course, I want to like what I write too, and I thoroughly enjoyed writing these stories.

In writing erotica/erotic romance, I'm always excited for the erotic journey! I'm on a path of sexual empowerment, enlightenment, and enjoyment. Thank you for reading this and I'm honored to be a part of your journey as well.

I am where I am because fans have responded to me and my content, so I owe everything to you! Thank you! Thank you! Thank you! You are a blessing in my life, and you give me more joy than you will ever know. I love interacting with all of you and I will never give that up.

My stories are erotica, so they have a generous amount of sex in them, as I believe our relationships should have as well. I hope you enjoyed this novella for what it is, literature that is in the erotica genre. It is very different from the romance genre, and there are different levels of heat in the erotica genre as well. Explore them all!

If you'd like more of my work, please see below for my list of published works on the following pages, visit my sexuality and erotica podcast, find my audiobooks, visit my website, my Patreon, visit my profile on Medium, and my linktree with all my links at https://linktr.ee/RuanWillow

Thank you for purchasing this book, I'd love to hear your thoughts in an honest review on the site where you purchased the book from. I'd absolutely love it if you shared my book with others. It warms my heart profusely when I see someone who has taken the time to review/share my book. Love you all very much!

All my best, yours truly, with overflowing love from a full heart,

Ruan Willow

Erotica author, sexuality/erotica podcaster, and erotic book narrator

Oh F*ck Yeah with Ruan Willow Podcast

It's free in audio on podcast apps, some video version on Spotify and YouTube at Ruan Willow Podcaster! Also airing on the internet radio station Full Swap Radio website and app Tuesdays and 6 pm CST, and Wednesdays 8 am (subject to change, check for the current schedule online) AND the PodNation TV Network/Roku TV/Fire TV powered by Podnation Pods anytime VOD on the app, and Sundays and Mondays After Dark Hours around 11 pm Eastern Time Zone (subject to change), watch it here: player frontlayer

Anthologies and Award Nominations

Ruan has stories in the following anthologies:
He Will Obey (which was AWARDED THE 2020 SILVER PIGTAIL IN BEST ANTHOLOGY CATEGORY
The Femdom Coven (nominee for 2021 Golden Pigtail Smut Awards)
Inside of Ruan Willow (also available in an audiobook)
(this audiobook was a nominee for the 2021 Golden Pigtail Smut Awards)

Decadent Erotica An Anthology **3rd Place Winner in the 2022 Golden Pigtails Smut Awards for Dark/Taboo Category**
Nominations for the 2023 Golden Pigtail Awards include:
Servicing the Trash Man, My Filthy Hotwife Adventure
Dressing Room Domme
Anthology Ruan has a story in titled Hearts and Flowers, Whips and Chains
Please vote for me! Wish me luck!

Other links:

Ruan Willow on Goodreads Ruan Willow Goodreads Author page[1]

Ruan Willow on BookBub https://www.bookbub.com/profile/ruan-willow

Sign up for Ruan's newsletter: https://subscribepage.io/ruanwillow

ARC copies are usually on BookSirens and StoryOrigin App. Check those sites for FREE ARC of books and audiobooks.

1. https://www.goodreads.com/author/show/21312130.Ruan_Willow

Don't miss out!

Visit the website below and you can sign up to receive emails whenever Ruan Willow publishes a new book. There's no charge and no obligation.

https://books2read.com/r/B-A-TOPT-XMRWC

BOOKS 2 READ

Connecting independent readers to independent writers.

Did you love *Friends With Benefits*? Then you should read *Decadent Erotica: An Anthology*[2] by Ruan Willow!

[3]

Decadent Erotica is an anthology to please your deepest desires. It's a book of ten erotic stories to quench your fantasies and will also satisfy, intrigue, and enflame your passion. This sexy book includes stories about a pleasure Dom with his sub where he's addicted to making her climax, a couple who succumbs to dark alley impromptu intimacy, naughty office oral fun between coworkers, sneaky and intense nighttime passion between a husband and wife, and a scorching hot coffee shop that pushes all the limits. Not only will those steamy tales light up your yummy alone reading time, but so will the short stories about taboo female domination, a morning filled with surprise skin-on-skin rubs, but also thong panties plucked from the kitchen cabinet as inspiration for intimate relations, and a threesome rendezvous in a dressing room where female-female-male means extreme pleasure taken while in semi-public. And last but not by any means least, excite yourself with an extremely hot orgy party story.Get this compilation of

---

2. https://books2read.com/u/mZEQvJ

3. https://books2read.com/u/mZEQvJ

steamy spicy short stories from Ruan Willow all in one book. She's an erotica author, podcaster at Oh F*ck Yeah with Ruan Willow, sex blogger & influencer, and NSFW audiobook narrator. Some of these stories are also narrated by Ruan on the podcast. Check out her podcast which is free on podcast apps.

Short story titles in this anthology:

FFM Dressing Room Hookup Rendezvous

Mallory and Derek Attend Their First Sex Party

His and Her Sleepfucking, Nighttime Passion, Getting Fucked into the Afterglow

Her Pleasure Dom

Dark Alley Sex

Getting Head at Work

A Morning Tit F*ck Sweetened a Dreaded Day

A Thong in the Kitchen Cupboard

The Licking Sip Coffee Shop

His Submission, She Dominated Him Out of a Speeding Ticket

Read more at https://ruanwillowauthor.com/.